STOWAWAY SLAVES

Other Gladiator Boy titles to collect:

STOWAWAY SLAVES

DAVID GRIMSTONE

Hodder
Children's
Books

A division of Hachette Children's Books

First published in Great Britain in 2009
by Hodder Children's Books

A Catalogue record for this book is available from
the British Library

ISBN: 978 0 340 97053 9

Typeset by Tony Fleetwood

Printed in the UK by CPI Bookmarque, Croydon, CR0 4TD

The paper and board used in this paperback by Hodder Children's Books are natural
recyclable products made from wood grown in sustainable forests.
The manufacturing processes conform to the environmental
regulations of the country of origin.

Hodder Children's Books
a division of Hachette Children's Books
338 Euston Road, London NW1 3BH
An Hachette UK company

www.hachette.co.uk

For Chiara Stone, my beautiful wife.

I would like to dedicate the entire Gladiator Boy *series to Terry Pratchett. There is no writer, living or dead, for whom I have greater respect. Thank you for everything.*

CONTENTS

ANCIENT ITALY

PREVIOUSLY IN GLADIATOR BOY

Decimus Rex has escaped Arena Primus in the company of a fellow slave, Olu Umbika. Together, the pair have managed to do what no one else has ever done – flee the clutches of Slavious Doom. However, with the overlord's evil servant in pursuit of them, it seems only a matter of time before they are recaptured.

CHAPTER I

THE ESCAPE

Slavious Doom was well known in Avellino, and not simply because his arena loomed over the little town like an angry giant. The overlord was famous for his cruelty, and there was much evidence of this in the tortured screams that regularly erupted from the arena floor.

Despite these fears, the townsfolk managed to go about their everyday lives, largely ignoring the fiendish activities that took place on their borders.

But now nothing could hide the army of arena guards that marched through the gates of Avellino and began barging their way into people's homes.

All over the town, muscled feet connected

with old doors, splintering weak wood and forcing it away from the frames.

Men, women and children were thrown aside like rag dolls as the guards, many of them expressionless and moving as though they were being controlled by a particularly ruthless puppet-master, overturned tables and chairs, ripped open bedding and ransacked cupboards in their efforts to find the escaped slaves.

Beneath the town, an even more frantic search was taking place . . .

The dogs raced along the tunnel, throwing up foul water all around them as their enormous paws sprang off the sewer floor. Despite all being part of the same pack, they were biting and clawing each other at every turn ... and only seemed to concentrate on their goal when the sewer opened up before them.

The guards who were supposed to be handling the dogs were in deep trouble, and they knew it. The pack had broken free soon after they'd entered the tunnels, breaking their leashes and wounding several of the guards in the process. Most of the dogs were deformed by years of savage beatings and the rest were simply deranged. If the escaped children were in the tunnels, they wouldn't survive an encounter with them ... and the guards had clear instructions from Doom to bring Decimus Rex back alive.

'Down there!' screamed the guard captain, a vein standing out on his neck as he splashed madly through the sewer. 'You with the sword – take the opposite tunnel! We need to get those dogs back NOW!'

The guards broke off in different directions, as the tortured howls of the dogs echoed in the distance.

'This is crazy,' said Olu, trying to cover his nose and mouth to avoid breathing in the tunnel's horrific stench. 'We're going to get caught and thrown into the dungeon like all the others. We'll never be heard from again!'

'Nah,' said Decimus turning to Olu with a wide smile on his face. 'The aqueduct is the LAST place they'll look. It would be different if we'd gone missing INSIDE the arena, but we didn't. They KNOW we scaled the walls so they'll be looking outside – they've probably raided half of Avellino by now. When that fails, they'll assume we're miles away! Besides, even if they do follow us down here, they'll never find us – this place is a maze!'

The two slaves hurried along the low

tunnel, trying to keep to one side to avoid splashing through the sludgy mix of filth and fetid water that rushed beneath them.

After a few seconds, Decimus stopped and threw back a hand to block Olu from overtaking him.

'What is it?' said the boy, his eyes scanning the tunnel ahead of them.

'A grate,' Decimus whispered, as voices became audible in the distance. 'It's the one we always passed in the tunnel when they led us out.'

'Damn it! That tunnel is always crawling with guards.'

Decimus nodded, and craned his neck to see around the bend in the tunnel. A shaft of light flowed from the grate and penetrated the gloom.

'It's going to be difficult to get around, so we need to choose our moment carefully.'

Decimus waited a few more seconds, then crawled around the bend. Olu took a deep breath, and followed. By the time he had negotiated the curve in the tunnel, Decimus was already fast approaching the grate and its revealing spear of light. Olu bunched his hands into fists in order to stop them from shaking; when Decimus moved through the light, he was almost afraid to watch. Then, in an instant, it was over . . . and Decimus was on the far side of the grate, beckoning Olu forward with one hand and raising a finger to his lips with the other.

There were voices directly above them

coming from two guards who had evidently avoided being recruited for the hunt but were spending hours talking about it.

Olu tried to block out their conversation as he crept along beneath them.

'What will Doom do if he finds 'em?' said one. 'Do you reckon he'll just continue the trials as normal?'

'He'll beat 'em both within an inch o' their lives,' said the other. 'He might even kill 'em, if he's . . . hey . . . what was that?'

Olu froze on the edge of the light stream. As far as he could tell, he hadn't made a sound. Nevertheless, the guards had evidently heard something. He hunkered down in the shadows on the edge of the grate and waited, still shaking with fear. On the far side of the light, Decimus had a troubled, questioning look on his face.

'Look lively,' said the first guard, above them. 'Someone's coming.'

The two guards fell silent as several shadows crossed the grate, blocking out the light as they went. Olu took the opportunity to make a dash for it, using the marching troops as cover. He reached Decimus just as the guards continued their conversation.

'That was Hain's lot, wasn't it? I wonder what they're doing here?'

'I think they've got attack dogs in the sewers. If you ask me, that's risk—'

Decimus and Olu didn't hear the end of the guard's sentence, as a sudden splash in the tunnel ahead caused them both to scramble back against the wall.

There, in the distant gloom, was a heavy-set guard. He'd dropped into the sewer via a grate further along the tunnel and was proceeding towards them.

'Back!' Olu whispered, frantically. 'We need to go back!'

'No,' Decimus shouted, grabbing his friend by the arm and driving him against the sewer wall. 'There's at least two guards above that grate!'

As his voice echoed loudly in the tunnel,

two things happened at once.

First, the guard in the tunnel ahead spotted them in the shadows and charged forward with a loud cry. Then, the grate above them was wrenched aside, and the two guards dropped into the sewer beside them.

Decimus scrambled backwards and slipped into the river of murky water, one hand clamped over his mouth. Olu simply froze where he was standing. Neither of them noticed that the sound of distant howling had grown steadily louder with every passing second.

'You boys stay right where you are,' warned the solitary guard, drawing his sword and holding it in front of him.

'I'd listen to him if I were you,' echoed one of the two guards behind the boys. 'We've got you now; don't make it worse by trying anything . . . foolish.'

Decimus gritted his teeth, and in that second Olu knew that his friend was about to do something very, very foolish indeed.

Without a single word of warning, Decimus made to charge at the two guards behind him. In the last split second, however, as they were raising their fists and preparing to tackle him, he suddenly changed direction and barrelled headfirst into the guard on the other side of

the tunnel. The boy
moved with such
speed that his
enemy was
taken
completely by
surprise, and the
pair crashed to the floor in a complicated
web of punches and kicks.

The howling in the tunnels reached fever
pitch, and even Olu was distracted from his
fear. He kicked himself away from the sewer
wall and took up a defensive stance,
seemingly inviting the two guards to attack.

Then the situation in the tunnel exploded
into chaos.

At first, Olu thought the guards had both

made a desperate lunge for him. It was only when they crashed into the water that he saw the dogs. They leapt upon the back of each guard, their slavering jaws working madly as they bit into every exposed piece of flesh they could find.

Olu leapt back and, turning on his heels, splashed through the tunnel towards Decimus and the remaining guard. Locking his hands together, he swung around with his elbow and glanced a well-aimed blow at the side of the guard's head. The big man, who had managed to overpower Decimus and was attempting to choke the young slave into unconsciousness, yelped as the blow sent a sharp pain through his neck . . . and released his grip. Decimus used the momentary

advantage to draw his legs back. Then, with
every ounce of strength he could muster, he
drove both feet squarely into the chest of
the guard. The heavy brute flew backwards,
just as a third rabid dog rounded the bend
in the tunnel. Olu flung himself flat,
plunging into the water as the monstrous
animal leapt over him and landed, in a hail
of spittle and filth, on the guard's
shoulders.

'Go!' Decimus screamed at the top of his voice, snatching up the big man's sword. 'Go! Go! Now!'

He and Olu thundered along the tunnel, taking every new passage they could find and trying to put as much distance between them and the hunting party as they could. Every few seconds they would splash to an abrupt halt as one of the savage dogs tore across a passage in front of them. Neither Olu nor Decimus had any doubt that the dogs would tear them limb from limb if their paths crossed.

They ran on, left, right, ahead, right again. 'Rats!' Olu cried, pointing to an army of giant vermin that spilled out from a junction up ahead. 'Look

at the size of them!' He collapsed
against the wall and, fighting to
catch his breath, he whispered,
'Which way should we go?'

'They're both dark and they both stink to
the heavens,' said Decimus. 'Which way did
those rats come from?'

'The passage on the left; why?'

'Rats go to the surface for food.
We were always seeing them around the
entrance, don't you remember?'

Olu nodded. 'Left it is, then.'

The two slaves peered into the new
passage, and then began to crawl into the
gloom. They hadn't taken more than a few
steps, however, when a pair of bright,
demented eyes flashed in front of them.

Pawing slowly out of the shadows, the dog snarled deeply; a low and guttural rasp that grew in pitch as it emerged into the meagre light of the junction.

Decimus raised the sword and, to Olu's astonishment, started to growl back. He also, very carefully, turned the sword around so that the blade was facing down, towards his feet and away from the animal.

'What are you doing?' said the stunned slave, taking several steps towards the junction. 'Have you gone mad? What—'

Decimus curled his lips so that his teeth and gums were bared. Then he drew in a deep breath and blew a powerful burst of air through his teeth, spraying saliva over the animal as the noise intensified.

'That will make it madder, you idiot!'

'Grrrrraaaaaaargh,' Decimus continued. 'Grraaargghhh!'

Olu knew the dog was going to leap before it happened, but it soon became apparent that Decimus knew it, too. Instead of diving aside or attempting to dodge the enraged animal, the slave stood his ground and only made his move at the moment when Olu was sure he was doomed.

Gripping the sword tightly in both hands, Decimus brought the pommel up with such ferocity that Olu heard the sickening crack inside his head seconds before he actually heard it in reality.

The pommel slammed into the slavering animal's jaw and it dropped to the ground like a sack of meat, hitting the water with a loud splash.

'Now we run,' Decimus whispered to Olu. 'And we don't stop running until we both collapse.'

CHAPTER
II

THE
WRATH

Drin Hain strode along the corridor, his black robes billowing out behind him. Slavious Doom's shadowy apprentice put many of the guards who served him in mind of a dark wraith, a hungry ghost who appeared on the battlements of abandoned castles, half demented and hungry for blood. An aura of icy calm surrounded him, and at times it seemed as though he could actually smell the fear in those he chose to question.

Today's unfortunate victim was a jailer called Truli. The man cowered before Hain, his eyes focused firmly on one of the figure's narrow shoulders. It was rumoured in the arena that Hain had been horribly burned as a child, and the sight of his face was something that, once seen, no man could ever forget. Truli was incredibly grateful that the hood concealed much of what lay within.

'Your ineptitude has allowed these slaves to escape,' said the rasping voice. 'Therefore, you will seek to avoid a painful death by following my every command WITHOUT question. Do you understand?'

Truli bowed his head.

'Anything you wish, I will do gladly,' he whispered. 'In the name and glorious mercy of our lord and master, the great Slavious Doo—'

'Take me to the dungeons.'

Truli quickly leapt to his feet and plucked a ring of keys from his belt.

'This way, master,' he said. 'Where would

you like to start? The cells are divided int—'

'Not the cells, Truli ... the DUNGEONS. Beneath the arena.'

'Y-yes, sir.' Truli moved off in an awkward series of limps, but seemed almost hesitant to comply with the orders. 'A v-very unusual request, master. I was always told NEVER to take people down the—'

'Your orders have changed.'

The jailer didn't say another word. Reaching the end of the corridor, he used his keys to open a vast iron portal that seemed to consist almost entirely of locks, bolts and chains. Eventually, the door was opened and Truli disappeared into the smoky depths beyond. Drin Hain dismissed his personal guards and followed the jailer down. The corridors below were dank but extremely well lit, with mounted braziers positioned at regular intervals on the ancient walls.

The two men walked in silence for a time, as two flights of steep and dusty steps gave way to a long sloping corridor that itself led into yet another subterranean stairwell. Eventually, the moans and wails of various tormented souls indicated that they were drawing near to the dungeons.

At length, the passage opened into a vast circular cave with several ropes hanging down from a pulley mechanism that sprouted from the ceiling. The ropes were attached to the floor, which itself appeared to be a giant disc of grated iron.

'Here we are, master. The Oubliette. This is where the current crop of failures are.'

Hain folded his arms. 'Open it.'

Several cries rang out from below as Truli moved over to a rusty-looking crank handle that stood proud of the wall and began to turn it in slow, deliberate circles. The ropes sprang to life, and the disc began, very slowly, to move.

Hain waited until the pit was half revealed before he made for the edge. There, glaring down at a horde of frightened, disturbed and half-despairing faces, he reached into his robe and produced a roll of battered parchment. As he did so, several of the boys cried out for mercy.

'You will be silent or I will command my guards to pour boiling pitch down upon you,' Hain snapped. 'You will also listen to me VERY carefully. I am about to read out several names from this list. If your name is called out, you will prepare to be drawn up from the pit in your chains. Then you will follow me. Those whose names are not called will remain – any attempt to escape will be met with death dealt swiftly by my hand. Anyone who doesn't fully understand my words can KEEP ON SHOUTING.'

Silence descended on the oubliette; scores of hopeful eyes turned upward.

Drin Hain unfurled the parchment and, to Truli's surprise, ordered a ladder to be lowered into the pit. Then he began to read out the names.

Several minutes later, a line of four boys were dragged through the dungeon catacombs. Each was connected to the others by a stout chain, so when one staggered and fell they were all pulled to the ground.

Drin Hain marched along ahead of the slaves, occasionally barking orders or requesting directions from jailer Truli, who knew the maze of tunnels better than anyone else.

When the group were finally clear of the dungeons and had emerged into the weak sunlight of the arena floor, Hain instructed his own guards to take over from Truli and the boys found themselves led into a part of the arena they were not at all familiar with. Several flights of stairs dropped away beneath them and, at length, they arrived at a grand doorway which overlooked most of the arena's vast interior: two sentry guards stood on duty outside.

Hain announced himself to one of the men, who nodded and led the group into a large and ornately decorated room. Plush red curtains hung from golden rails and several statues occupied the floor space between the door and a raised dais that supported a great arched throne. Upon the throne sat a man the slaves recognized immediately.

Slavious Doom was an imposing figure, his dark hair and beard framing a face that never looked anything less than pure evil. He didn't get up from the throne when the slaves were paraded before him.

'Drin?' he said, an enquiring expression on his face. 'What is the meaning of all this? Unless I am very much mistaken, these are NOT the escaped slaves I ordered you to find ...'

Hain inclined his head slightly.

'Kicking down doors and raiding houses are jobs for brainless servants, my lord. Your guards have already been dispatched to search Avellino. In fact, I understand the slaves evaded them in the sewers beneath the town. They are faster and smarter than we suspected, and will be halfway across Campania in a matter of days. My time is better spent elsewhere...'

He turned to indicate the line of boys beside him, some of whom were barely able to stand.

'On your left, my lord, we have Ruma, the Etrurian and Argon the Gaul. Then we have Teo and, on his right, Gladius the Calabrian.

My spies inside the arena inform me that these slaves were all close companions of Decimus Rex and the boy Olu. They were seen talking together during the trials, and they all shared a section in the holding cells.'

Doom's expression remained cold. 'And?' he snapped. 'What of it?'

'My plan is to announce the execution of these boys, at a memorable location, with a second announcement that their fate can be altered if Decimus and his friend hand themselves in to our guard patrols. Suvius Tower will be a good strong location, as it is visible for miles around. We can stage the executions there, but also lie in wait for the young . . . heroes.'

As a wave of comprehending horror

washed over the gathered slaves and they began to dart terrified glances at each other, Drin Hain continued to outline his plan.

'I have it on good authority that the Calabrian was closest to Decimus during the trials. Therefore, his execution alone should bring Decimus out of hiding; the others will be . . . a bonus entertainment. I take it that all of these children are expendable, my lord?'

A sick smile spread across Doom's sharp features.

'They are indeed, Drin,' he said. 'They are indeed. Your thinking, as always, is inspired. You may proceed with your plan.'

CHAPTER
III

THE
HARBOUR

Decimus and Olu had been
travelling through the
aqueducts for three days,
feeding on the sort of scraps that even the
rats wouldn't touch and sleeping beside
rivers filled with the foulest stench
imaginable. At one point they had come
upon a vast network of different tunnels
but, without the slightest clue as to which
way they should travel, they ended up
selecting their path largely at random.

However, finally, it seemed that they had
hit a lucky break.

'It's a harbour,' said Olu squeezing his
face against the bars of the wall-mounted
grate they had found. 'I can see five, six,
maybe even seven ships! We

can escape, we can get away from Doom! Haha! This is fantastic!'

'I agree,' Decimus muttered. 'The only problem is that we don't actually have the first idea about where we are. Those ships could be going ANYWHERE!'

'So?' Olu looked amazed at his friend's attitude. 'Anywhere is better than the arena, surely?'

'I want to go home, Olu . . . and considering that my home is in Tarentum, there's a good chance we're going in exactly the WRONG direction.'

Olu turned to face his friend; his expression was stern.

'You can't go home, Decimus. Not now; probably not ever. Our parents got us into this, remember? Your trials are paying for your father's debts. Don't you think Doom's warriors are likely to be keeping a constant watch on your home town? Going back to Tarentum right now is just unthinkable. We need to get as far away from Doom as possible: we must get beyond his reach.'

Decimus fought back the urge to argue; he knew deep down that Olu was right. There really was no going back home – at least, not yet.

Returning his attention to the grate, Decimus put both his hands around the bars and beckoned for Olu to do the same.

'Do you think we can wrench this off?' he muttered. 'I think it would be better to go now, under cover of darkness, than to wait until morning light. The entire harbour will probably be crawling with merchants by then.'

Olu nodded, closed his own fists around the grate, and gave it an experimental tug.

'It feels pretty sturdy to me,' he admitted.
'Let's both pull on a count of three. One, two, three, GO!'

The two slaves heaved on the bars with all their might, but the grate didn't give an inch.

'We need to find another way out,' Decimus muttered. 'There's no other choice. We'll just have to go back to the last set of steps we passed and up through the opening beside that caved-in section of tunnel.'

'Yeah, but we can't – that would take us right on to the streets . . .'

'So? We'll have to brave them.'

Olu spun around.

'Are you crazy?' he gasped. 'We'll be spotted in minutes!'

'Do you have a better idea? Besides, it's

dark outside – that should give us half a chance. C'mon!'

It was dark in the coastal town of Formiae, and a gentle breeze was blowing. The guard patrols on these narrow streets were few and far between, partly because there was seldom any trouble that the locals couldn't sort out but mostly because even the most dedicated watchmen could be persuaded from their duties by sounds of merriment and offers of free wine. Moreover, the kind of fights that started in harbour towns between drunken sailors soon turned into large scale brawls that most common guards would do anything to avoid if at all possible.

Decimus and Olu had been watching a particularly loud and obnoxious pair for the best part of an hour. Their duties seemed to consist of walking up and down the main harbour stretch, glancing occasionally at the line of mostly unmanned ships and then falling into the first drinking pit they passed for a ten-minute break.

'They're back,' Olu whispered, pointing to a doorway some distance from their hiding place in the gardens of a small temple overlooking the harbour. 'As soon as they get "distracted" again, we can make our move . . . hang on, they're going inside.'

'Right,' said Decimus, but he wasn't really paying attention to the guards: his eyes were fixed on the long shadows being cast by the impressive collection of ships that dominated the harbour before them.

'I wish I knew where we were,' he muttered.

Olu hadn't taken his own eyes from the lighted doorway.

'We're somewhere on the border of Latium,' he said.

'What?' Decimus turned to his friend, visibly shocked at the revelation. 'How can you possibly know that?'

'I don't,' Olu admitted. 'I'm guessing, but I've been to Latium before – a place called Caieta – and the guard's armour was very similar. I reckon we crossed the border between Campania and Latium while we were in the aqueduct. Decimus . . . '

Olu reached over and slapped the young slave on the shoulder.

'What?'

'They've gone back in: time for us to move!'

The two friends detached themselves from the temple garden and began to run for the nearest ship, ducking and rolling several times when a doorway opened and a party of drunken sailors endeavoured to make the short trip between the drinking pits.

Scrabbling in the dirt, Olu managed to drag himself behind a small collection of barrels mere seconds before one of the sailors made a loud and worrying remark to his companions.

'What was that?'

Three of the revellers continued to stagger towards the next inn, but one wandered over to join his swaying mate.

'I heard something; reckon I saw something, too.'

Olu tried to peer out from his new hiding place without attracting any attention, but he couldn't see Decimus anywhere. Still, he thought, with any luck those two drunken idiots can't see him either.

'Thieves, I'll bet: tryin' to get on ship.'

The first sailor began to lurch in Olu's direction. His companion made to do the same, but quickly collapsed into the dirt. As Olu slowly moved himself even further behind the barrels, he saw the prone sailor flop about in the dirt and attempt to get up several times before the effects of the drink overcame him.

Unfortunately, the same could not be said for the first, who was advancing on Olu's position with surprising speed and now seemed to be armed with a short sword. He had to get away.

Olu leapt to his feet and ran, but he stumbled across a barrel that had fallen over behind the others and crashed to the ground in a heap. The sailor was on him in seconds.

'You there! Hold up, thief!'

The sailor charged forward, but Decimus emerged from the shadows like a demon, clearing the barrels in one swift jump and landing heavily on the big man's back. Olu looked on in horror as Decimus snatched hold of the sailor's head and twisted it with all his might. The sword clattered to the ground, and the sailor hit the dirt with a dull thud.

'W-what-what—'

'You'd have preferred he ran you through with his blade?' Decimus snapped. 'Now come on, we need to move him before that other one wakes up, and then we must get on a ship!

There's no time for shock, do you hear me? There's no TIME!'

Olu raced after his friend, the scene playing over and over in his mind. He couldn't believe how strong Decimus had grown since they'd met on the first day at the arena. Evidently, the numerous trials, battles and ferocious combats had turned his friend into a formidable warrior. Together, they made for the nearest ship, dragging the corpse of the sailor along with them and trying to keep to the shadows.

'Leave him there,' Olu whispered, as he and Decimus deposited their victim behind an untidy heap of tangled fishing nets. 'With any luck, they won't find him until morning.'

Decimus nodded, returning his attention

to the ships in the harbour.

'The third along,' he said. 'That's the one we need to get on. I was watching them all from the temple garden, and the others have skeleton crews still manning them. I haven't seen any movement on the third one at all.'

'What type of ship is it?' Olu hazarded, squinting at the distant shape. 'I'm useless at ships: don't know the first thing about them.'

'Me neither,' Decimus admitted. 'But it doesn't really matter – the only thing that matters is whether or not we get discovered on board. So let's find ourselves a good hiding place.'

'You can try, boys,' said a voice behind them. 'But not before we've handed you into the guards and made some nice Denarii.'

Decimus and Olu both turned very slowly, but they couldn't see anyone around them. A grim silence settled in the shadows as the two slaves looked left and right, down at their feet and, finally, up at the ship that was

outlined above them.

Unfortunately, they saw the two smiling pirates leaning over the deck of the ship too late to avoid the net that was quickly dropped on top of them.

Olu struggled wildly with the heavy ropes, but Decimus knew enough about fishing nets to know that struggling would just get them more entangled, so he relaxed and quickly urged Olu to do the same.

A few seconds later, the pirates were standing beside them, their eyes reflecting the gleam of coins they could already imagine filling their pockets.

'Up,' said the first pirate, dragging Decimus and Olu on to their feet. 'Me and me mate here will share your reward money . . . the others'll be sorry they went ashore when they see what they missed out on.'

'Slump down,' Decimus whispered to Olu. 'Make yourself as heavy as possible – dead weight! Dead weight!'

The first pirate soon realized he didn't have the strength to lift the net and both boys together, so he motioned to his companion to help. Combining their efforts, they managed to drag the pair upright, but not before Decimus had used the delay to loop one square in his own part of the net over the giant mooring ring that tethered the boat to the harbour.

'Move!'

The pirates dragged Decimus and Olu forward, but soon realized that they couldn't progress any further than a few feet. The larger of the two men immediately assumed that Decimus was holding himself back; he reached through the net and grasped the young slave by his throat, shaking him vigorously before moving on to Olu and repeating the action.

'NOW MOVE YOURSELVES!' he boomed, as the other pirate joined him in a renewed effort to drag them away.

Again, the boys staggered a short distance before coming to an abrupt and immovable halt.

'Net must be snagged on something,' said the first, but as he went back to investigate Decimus grabbed his arm through the net and threw all his weight into the man. Sensing the point of the attack, Olu charged into his friend's back, giving the young slave enough momentum to drive the pirate over the edge of the quay. The big man toppled backwards and plummeted between the ship and quay, with Decimus and Olu tumbling after him. Realizing that his companion and the highly valuable slaves were all going over the edge, the second pirate dived after them,

grabbing the end of the net and being dragged along for the ride.

The first pirate met a terrible fate; he had fallen on to a pole that jutted from the water and had been completely impaled . . . a horrific expression settled on his face as the boys struggled far above him.

Decimus and Olu were caught in the net, which spelled both good and bad news for them. The good news was that Decimus had hooked the net firmly to the mooring ring, so there was no chance of them falling. The bad news was that the second pirate had managed to hang on to the outside of the net, and had produced a dagger which he was using in an attempt to cut through the ropes.

'Punch him!' Decimus cried at Olu, trying to spur his friend into action. 'Shake him off, damn it!'

'I can't!' Olu yelled, moving his arm as the pirate's knife-blade missed the rope and cut into him. 'I can just about hold on as it is!'

Decimus let go of his side of the net and leaped on to Olu's back. The skinny slave gasped in surprise and fought to hold on to the ropes as Decimus climbed over him and, grasping the net tightly in both hands, drove himself forward and slammed his forehead into the face of the struggling attacker.

A spray of blood flew from the pirate's nose, and he dropped the dagger. This time, however, Olu's reactions were just as quick as those of his friend. The slave reached through the net, caught the dagger and plunged it into the leg of the pirate.

'Argghhhh! You little—'

He didn't finish the curse; Decimus slammed a fist into his jaw and he fell into the water, striking his head on the quayside as he fell before sinking beneath the waves.

Decimus faltered for a moment and lost his grip on the net, but Olu grabbed hold of him.

'Wh-what now?' the skinny slave whispered.

Decimus took a few seconds to catch his breath.

'We cut ourselves out of here and climb

back on to the quay,' he muttered. 'Then we should try and sneak aboard the third ship, like we planned; I certainly don't fancy taking on more pirates from *that* crew.'

CHAPTER IV

THE SUVIUS TOWER

Argon the Gaul looked down at his bruised, swollen wrists, and winced. A series of ropes, chains and buckles had taken their toll on his flesh, and they conspired with the scars and burns on his back to form a detailed map of agony.

He looked across at the others, but they all seemed equally pained and exhausted. Teo was picking some dirt from his toenails, Ruma was scratching at one of the walls with a tiny shard of splintered wood and Gladius was slumped in a corner, scratching his belly and moaning about Decimus and Olu betraying them all.

'Oh shut up, will you?' Argon snapped, struggling to his feet and stomping over to the room's heavily barred window. 'I'm sick and tired of hearing about it. They've escaped, OK?

Good for them. It's not their fault Slavious Doom's bloodhound has a sick sense of humour – I mean, how could they possibly know he'd do something like this? Besides, you're always changing your mind about Decimus – one minute he was your best friend and the next he's stabbed us all in the back – make up your mind, will you?'

'Do you really think Hain will execute us?' said Ruma. The Etrurian had been silent for most of the morning, so his words drew immediate glances from Gladius and Teo.

'Of course he will,' Argon confirmed. 'The man's a monster, or a lunatic, or worse.'

'Yeah,' said Gladius, sulkily. 'Some of the stories about his brutality have to be made up, though: surely no one can be THAT bad?'

'You're willing to bet your life, are you?'
Argon muttered. 'What's left of it, anyway . . .'

Teo stopped picking at his feet, and cast a
doubtful expression at the Gaul.

'What's wrong with him?' said Argon.

Gladius shrugged. 'He probably doesn't
understand what's happening.'

'Yeah,' Argon agreed. 'Well, that will
change when Hain marches in here and runs
us all through with his sword.'

Teo suddenly scrambled to his feet and
crossed the room in two long strides. Argon
stepped back instinctively, but Teo hurried
past him and moved to stand beside the
window.

'. . . Where . . .' he said, pronouncing the
word as if it was the most complicated thing

he'd ever had to say, '... are ... we ... ?'

Argon, Ruma and Gladius all shared glances in the stunned silence. Apart from his name, these were the first words Teo had ever spoken to them.

It was Gladius who answered.

'We're in a place called the Suvius Tower,' he said. 'It's about five miles from the coast of Campania. They brought us here last night, in the cart with all the chains. Do you remember? Do—'

'Of course he does,' Ruma interrupted. 'He's foreign; he's not stupid. How do you know where we are, anyway?'

Gladius heaved himself off the dusty floor and padded over to the window. The view was mostly flat land, punctuated in places by the odd town or the outline of a distant city.

'I heard the guards talking when we were in the cart,' he continued. 'YOU all fell asleep.'

'I've heard of the Suvius Tower,' said Ruma, a dark expression on his face. 'It's a place for . . . big events. People come from miles around to watch.'

'By big events you mean executions, right?' Argon spat. 'C'mon – at least have the guts to say it.'

Ruma glared at him.

'FINE. I was just trying not to dwell on the bad stuff, OK?'

'Whatever,' said Gladius, with a dismissive shrug. 'We're all doomed anyway.'

The door flew open at that moment, causing all of the gathered slaves to step back very warily.

Three guards entered the room, making way for a short and gaunt-looking jailer who marched in wearing the sort of spiteful expression the boys had come to recognize in many of Doom's servants.

'I have news for you,' he said, his words dripping with poisonous undertones. 'The great Slavious Doom and his honourable servant Drin Hain have decided that you will each die in an interesting and entertaining manner, for the amusement of his lord's guests. In three days' time . . .'

He looked around the room, his eyes finding Ruma, then Teo and finally Argon, before they came to rest upon Gladius.

'One of you will be thrown from the top of this very tower . . .'

The little jailer allowed his message to bleed into the minds of his audience before he continued. 'After that, another of you will be dropped into one of several cages. The cages will be covered, so you will not know your fate until it is upon you. We currently have a wonderful selection of lions, snakes, sharks and crocodiles . . . so, once again, entertainment for Lord Doom's guests will be assured.'

All four slaves managed to hold the jailer's gaze, not one of them giving the little man the satisfaction of seeing their fear.

'Then, when only two of you remain, one shall be hung on a scaffold in the square at the base of this very tower. The other . . .' he hesitated slightly, another cruel smile spreading across his face like treacle, 'will have the honour of being executed in traditional style by the hand of Drin Hain himself . . . in a duel of mortal combat.'

The jailer started to laugh, but he was quickly interrupted by Argon.

'Who gets what?' he snapped. 'Are we allowed to know which of us will go first?'

The jailer smiled again, his jackal features creasing up so his face was consumed by folds of loose flesh.

'You will all find out at the appointed time . . . and then you will be able to watch one another suffer!'

He turned and made to leave the room, pausing briefly in the doorway and casting a sly glance back at the group.

'Unless your friends give themselves up, of course,' he muttered.

Ruma, Argon, Teo and Gladius watched as the group paraded out of the room and slammed the door behind them. The jailer's cackle still echoed through the tower several minutes after the spiteful little wretch had departed.

CHAPTER
V

HIDING
OUT

The ship had departed shortly before dawn. Decimus knew this because there were slivers of light penetrating the hiding place he and Olu had found upon boarding it. Unfortunately, the space behind the captain's cabin soon proved to be a busy spot and so they'd decided to relocate elsewhere. Now they were hunkered down in the bilge, wedged between stinking barrels and chests that smelled like they were full of rotting fish.

'Did you notice those benches on the deck above?' Decimus whispered, pulling Olu away from a potentially noisy rack of chains.

'What?' came the hushed reply. Olu shook himself from his reverie. 'Yes, I saw them . . . and the oars. This is a

slave ship,
Decimus. You
know what that means?'

'Yeah,' said the young warrior, with a grim
smile. 'It means that if we start trouble while
we're on board, we'll have the slavers
outnumbered.'

When Olu looked up sharply, his eyes
wide and his jaw gaping, Decimus quickly
raised a hand.

'Relax, Olu. I know we can't afford to be
captured on here.'

The other slave smiled, and a flood of
relief washed over him.

'I'm not like you, Decimus,' he said. 'I
don't think I can do this much longer. I'm
so very tired, and my bones feel like

they're crumbling.'

'You're doing well, Olu. Just remember, if it wasn't for you, we would never have escaped from the arena. You SAVED us. It's my turn now – whatever we do next, I will make it happen. I just need you to go along with me. Shhh – someone's coming!'

The two slaves crawled deeper into the

shadows as a pair of sweaty-looking galley
slavers clambered down the steps and began
to stalk around the bilge.

'C'mon,' said one. 'We'd better get this
barrel up or the Captain will make us row in
place o' the slaves . . . like he did last week
when old Reeky cheeked him.'

'It was hard going, that was,' said the other

spitting on the floor and cracking his knuckles. 'I don't know how those skinny scrapers manage it.'

'They get whipped if they don't row. They get no food if they don't row. They get drowned if they don't row. THAT is how they manage it. Besides, it was hard because there were only eight of us; there's forty of them! We should get to Suvius Tower with time to spare, I reckon.'

'Why do we keep going back there, anyway? Hain's lot never buy more than a handful of the old sots we pick up.'

'Yeah, yeah – now help me out.'

Together they lifted a barrel from the bilge and began to heave it towards the steps. After dropping the load several times, the two slavers eventually managed to get it on to the deck above, and had soon scrambled after it. As the second one disappeared through the gap, a scroll fell from his tunic and landed in a puddle of dirty bilge water.

Once the slavers were gone, the shadows seemed to return, creeping around the huddled pair like spears of black mist. The drip, drip, drip of a thousand tiny leaks echoed throughout the bilge.

‘Did you hear that?’ Decimus whispered. ‘They’re going to trade with Drin Hain . . . and there’s only a handful of them! Can you believe that?’

'Don't even think about it,' said Olu. 'The eight slavers are probably built like Roman fortresses with muscles like granite and the forty slaves are probably all starving skeletons with diseases who lack the will to live. Wait here a second . . . I see something.'

Olu crawled around the perimeter of the bilge and crouched beside the steps. Glancing over his shoulder at Decimus, he put a thin finger to his lips. Then he picked up the wet scroll that lay in a small puddle of bilge water beside the hatch and scampered back to where Decimus was hiding.

'One of the slavers dropped it,' he panted. 'It might be orders or something. I can't read it, though. You'll have to tell me what it says.'

Decimus rolled his eyes, and began to scan

the parchment. Even in the shadows, Olu saw the look of horror slowly consume his friend's tired face. The young slave swallowed a few times, but didn't reply. He looked up at Olu, then down at the scroll once again.

'What IS it? Tell me!' urged Olu.

Decimus stretched the scroll to its full length, and glared at the words that were burning into his eyes as they followed each line of text.

'It's a notice,' he said aloud. 'It says: *News on escaped slaves, Decimus Rex and Olu Umbika.* There's a description of us both; pretty accurate, I'd say.'

Olu nodded, gloomily. 'Doom has a reputation,' he said. 'He and Hain will NEVER stop looking for us. They'll track us down until—'

'Listen to this,' said Decimus, with a grimace. '*To ensure the full attention of the two slaves we have arranged a series of four private executions for the night of the 24th at Suvius Tower in Southern Campania. Those scheduled for execution are the cellmates of Decimus Rex and Olu Umbika; the executions will only be cancelled if their friends hand themselves in to us. Should this fail to occur, we can guarantee a night of brutal entertainment for those with money and a taste for violence. Price of entry: 100 Denarii.*'

Olu remained silent for a long time. It was Decimus who managed to speak first.

'We can't let this happen,' he said. 'The 24th is tomorrow night, by my calculation. They're doing this because of us! Gladius, Argon, Ruma, Teo: they're all going to suffer and die because we escaped.'

Olu shook his head. 'It's a plan to draw us out! Surely you can see that?'

'It doesn't matter!' Decimus snapped. 'Whether it's a plan or not, we both know Doom and his twisted servant will go through with it! They don't CARE about Gladius or Ruma, or any of them. You don't have to go back, Olu ... but I must: I wouldn't have got through half of those trials if it wasn't for Gladius and the others. I can't let them die for me, Olu: I just can't.'

Olu shook his head, sadly. 'You really

think they would do the same for you, if the situation was reversed?'

Decimus shrugged. 'That doesn't matter – I can only think for myself, not for others. I was told that a long time ago, and it's true. Whether they could leave me to my death is for them to decide should they ever need to – but, right now, the decision is mine.'

Olu nodded and lowered his head. For a long time, Decimus was afraid his exhausted friend might burst into tears or simply curl up and sleep. At length, however, the slave raised his head once again, and Decimus spotted the familiar look of deep, determined thought on Olu's weathered face.

'Then we go back in force,' he muttered, gritting his teeth. 'The Suvius Tower is on a rock that juts out over the coast. If this ship has been there before, we have the perfect weapon. Hain's slave-traders won't be expecting an attack.'

'An attack?' Decimus repeated, wearing a puzzled expression. He almost didn't recognize the boy now standing in front of him from the tired figure he'd escaped with.

'A major attack,' Olu confirmed. 'We don't go back and just hand ourselves in – we storm the tower. Of course, we'll need to free the other slaves on this ship.' Olu climbed to his feet, using a barrel for support. 'To do that, we need a master key to their chains. Then we can take out the slavers and gain control. There were enough swords in the captain's cabin to give everyone on board at least two each.' He turned to Decimus, who was looking surprised and impressed by his friend's sudden determination.

'The big question,' Olu continued, 'is whether or not you think we can lead a horde of mutinous slaves on to victory? I wouldn't even think about trying it, myself – but after seeing you in those sewer tunnels, Decimus, I reckon you can do anything.'

Decimus turned to his friend, but the smile soon drained away from his face. As he peered over Olu's shoulder, a hatch at the other end of the ship was suddenly flung open, and a strangled cry erupted from the deck above . . .

COMING SOON

The Shadow of Doom has a sick sense of humour and is using Decimus and Olu's friends in a deadly game of cat and mouse. Can the boys capture the slave ship they are hiding on and make it back to the Suvius Tower in time to rescue their friends. The odds are stacked against them. Find out if they make it in . . .

THE REBELS' ASSAULT

ARENA COMBAT

Get ready to challenge your friends! Each Gladiator Boy book will contain a different trial – collect them all to run your own Arena of Doom – either at home or in the school playground.

TRIAL 3
THE HIDDEN

Decimus and Olu spend most of this book in hiding, but how good are you at concealment? This trial is all about hiding things in clever places where no one would think of to look.

You will need three players, one to play the shadow-lord Drin Hain and one to play the escaped slaves, Decimus and Olu.

Each hider (ie. one playing Decimus & one playing Olu) must select a distinctive stone or pebble and show it to the seeker (Drin Hain). The seeker must close his eyes and turn away from the other players. He must then count to 100. While he is counting, the hiders must conceal their objects somewhere nearby.

The seeker then goes in search of the objects, scoring one point for finding each and three points for finding both. He has a time limit of 20 minutes, which can be monitored with a watch.

If the seeker fails to find an item, the player that concealed it receives two points.

Play then revolves until everyone has been Decimus, Olu and Drin Hain once.

One character profile can be found on the next two pages and there will be more in the other Gladiator Boy books.

IMPORTANT RULES

The game must be played in a safe place and hiding places that are high up or dangerous are immediately disqualified and will score no points for remaining unfound.

The players must hide their stones within sight of the seeker, meaning that if they were to reveal their items they would be seen immediately. If they go beyond sight of the seeker, their items are disqualified.

The player with the most points at the end of the game is declared the winner!

CHARACTER PROFILE
TEO

NAME: Teo

FROM: The Orient

HEIGHT: 1.67 metres

BODY TYPE: Slender

BEST FRIEND: Ruma

CELLMATE: Argon

TEO QUIZ: How well do you know Teo? Can you answer the following three questions?

1. WHERE IS TEO WHEN HE IS SEEN PICKING DIRT FROM HIS TOE-NAILS?

2. WHEN TEO CHARGES AT AN ARCHED WINDOW, WHO THINKS HE IS CHARGING IN FOR A FIGHT?

3. APART FROM HIS NAME, WHAT ARE TEO'S FIRST WORDS IN THE GLADIATOR BOY SERIES?

Answers: 1. Sivius Tower, page 74 2. Argon, page 76/77
3. 'Where are we?', page 76

WEAPON PROFILE PIRATE WEAPONS

In a previous weapon profile, we looked at various swords. The pirates described in this book would have used something a little different. They would have used a special sort of sword called a 'cutlass'.

THE CUTLASS

The cutlass is very similar to a sword, but with one major difference – it has a curved blade. The cutlass was used on many ships because of its ability to cut through thick ropes ... vital when you're caught in a storm and need to sever the sails!

THE BOARDING AXE

The boarding axe was a special, long-handled axe that pirates used to break down the cabin doors of ships they boarded. There was also another version of the boarding axe; a short-handled one that was used when pirates leapt from one ship to another and slid down the sails, ripping them open as their axes bit through the material. (This latter variety may have existed only in fictional stories and films about pirates, but it's certainly an amazing sight to watch!)

READ MORE OF DECIMUS REX'S ADVENTURES IN BOOK FOUR OF THE GLADIATOR BOY SERIES:

THE REBELS' ASSAULT

Ruma, Argon, Teo and Gladius were led down from their cell at the top of Suvius Tower, dragged by the jailer's guards with such force that several cuts and bruises were earned along the way. At one point, Gladius stumbled and fell headlong down a flight of steps in the tower courtyard. However, rather than stop his momentum, the guards simply laughed and one even gave him an experimental kick to see if he would keep going.

By the time the group reached the gates of the fortress they had stored enough hatred for their captors to last several lifetimes.

In the courtyard, an eerie silence reigned. The guards assembled the slave line with a series of grunts and shoves. Then they withdrew, making space for the arrival of the spindly, gnome-like jailer who had so gleefully given the prisoners news of their pending executions. He climbed a wooden ladder beside the gates and hurried along a platform that spanned the gap just under the great archway. The slave line followed his progress and their eyes came to rest on the recognizable form of Drin Hain, draped in his trademark black robes and hood. The jailer cupped a hand to his face and whispered something to the wraith-like figure . . .

GLADIATOR BOY

Check out the Gladiator Boy website for games, downloads, activities, sneak previews and lots of fun! You can even get extra pieces of the arena and fantastic action figures! Sign up to the newsletter to receive exclusive extra content and the opportunity to enter special competitions.

WWW.GLADIATORBOY.COM

LET BATTLE COMMENCE!

MAKE YOUR OWN ARENA OF DOOM

1. Carefully cut around the outline of the arena section. Ask an adult to help if necessary.
2. Fold across line A. Use a ruler to get a straight edge.
3. Fold across line B. Use a ruler to get a straight edge.
4. Ask an adult to help you score along lines C & D with a pair of sharp scissors.
5. Fold up over line E and push the window out.
6. Repeat instructions 1 to 5 for every Arena of Doom piece collected.
7. Glue the top of each tab and stick them to the next piece of the arena. Repeat as necessary.

CHECK OUT THE WEBSITE FOR A PHOTO OF THE COMPLETE ARENA.

TO MAKE YOUR ACTION FIGURE

1. Cut around the outline of the figure. Ask an adult to help if necessary.
2. Cut along slot X at the bottom of the figure.
3. Cut out Gladiator Boy rectangle.
4. Cut along slot Y.
5. Slot figure into slot Y.